LETTERS
TO WENDY'S

LETTERS
TO WENDY'S

Joe Wenderoth

Verse Press
Athens, GA · Amherst, MA

Library of Congress Cataloging-in-Publication Data
Wenderoth, Joe.
  Letters to Wendy's / by Joe Wenderoth. — 1st ed.
    p. cm.
  ISBN 0-9703672-0-1
  I. Title.
  PS3573.E515 L47 2000
  813'.54 — dc21

                                        00-011569

Printed in the United States of America

14 13 12 11 10 9

TELL US ABOUT YOUR VISIT

WE CARE!

JULY 1, 1996

I had such a wonderful *meal*, in every sense of the word. I especially liked the *ordering* of the food. It asserts an altogether proper dominance. And how do you manage to hire such attractive people!! Often I visit Wendy's just to take a gander at your employees. Thank you! (for being there)

July 2, 1996

Today was awful. I don't know what happened—yesterday was great. I can't pin-point any single problem with the visit. There was just a kind of pall, an unasked-for strictness undermining the assumption of good will and cleanliness. Sometimes I love to linger in the ring of that strictness, of course, but why today was this love of lingering not possible?

JULY 3, 1996

Today I bought a small Frosty. This may not seem significant, but the fact is: I'm lactose intolerant. Purchasing a small Frosty, then, is no different than hiring someone to beat me. No different in essence. The only difference, which may or may not be essential, is that, during my torture, I am gazing upon your beautiful employees.

July 4, 1996 (Independence Day)

I wonder what "beauty" really is. I know that the little girl, Wendy, who is pictured on your cups and bags, is beautiful, and so is the green green descent into the valley. Within this descent, I can feel the overpowering order within which I am but a temporary eccentricity. This overpowering, anticipated but absent, is beauty. I'd like to spank Wendy's white ass and fuck her hard.

July 5, 1996

Today there was no blood in my stool. The sun was shining as I sat with my burger and Coke and gazed out across the parking lot. *Gazed*—there is the place where *what is* feels itself slipping—with difficulty—into the fitful sleep of replica. I did not gaze. I was the sleep *what is* gazed through. One is confused, though, having truly shit.

July 6, 1996

I was so high on Sudafed and whiskey today that I couldn't eat. I got a Coke—actually five Cokes, as I could refill for free. It's times like this—dehydrated, exhausted, unable to imagine home—that your plastic seats, your quiet understandable room, set beside but not quite overlooking the source of real value, offer me a tragedy small enough to want to endure.

July 10, 1996

The great thing about Wendy's—*one* of the great things—
is that no one ever has sex in this space. It's like sex is too
selfish an activity to go on here. To be in Wendy's is to
understand that there can be no *one* other; it is to disabuse
oneself of that foolish hope, and thereby resume the animal
in its more lonely, more mobbed mode of comportment.

July 11, 1996

The glamorous pictures of new items are possessed of such a tiny energy. Massive success accomplishes itself in tiny energy growing tinier. What is it that chooses to remain outside of this increasingly tiny energy—can we even give a name to such a freakish presence? The only time I love the other customers is when they seem, above all, to be eating.

JULY 12, 1996

I often think about over-eating. It's strange that I never have.
Each bite of my mustard-only double-cheeseburger is *so*
good that I reel in the aftermath. The meaty goodness
obliterates as much as it secures. I'm a fleshy bell, incapable
of vibrating any more vigorously. If I rang out with any more
force I don't know that I would remain a bell—and I don't
know that the air could stand me.

JULY 13, 1996

Today I was looking hard at Wendy. I felt like a doctor. I felt like Wendy was very ill, and no one could see it but me. That smile is the smile of a sexy girl who is well taken care of, but care, as we all know, is a relatively new hobby, and Wendy is already moving outside of its novelty. I like to dream that she will come to me for futile treatments.

JULY 14, 1996

It's amazing how I recognize the parking lot but do not recognize the parking lot's power to make customers appear. How is it that this place remains unfulfilled by its sudden natives? And why *these* natives, and not *those*? And what sort of homeland is so consistently oblivious to the tranquil violence of oh-so-similar orders following one another into merely wanting words?

July 16, 1996

Today I bought a salad just to look at it, smell it, rub it on my face. Again I'm feeling like a doctor, but now the feeling is clearer—I feel like an ancient doctor, with ancient ideas about what need be done. I asked the register-girl if it would be possible to have small holes drilled into my skull so that good strong coffee could be poured down on to my brain.

JULY 17, 1996

It feels good to be punched in the face, but only for an instant. This is what I was thinking as I sat in this afternoon's empty dining room. Then my mind wandered and I imagined Wendy was in my car with me. She said, "I'd like you to take your fat tongue and run it from my asshole to my clit over and over again." I said, "I'd like you to punch me in the face." Thus it ran, the empty dining room filling.

JULY 18, 1996

Today I felt like a cup of soda that had been sitting—
full—for too long. Watery, sides melting, barely able to
be handled—but *there*, so very very *there*, and simply
demanding proper disposal. It is my suspicion that,
however persuasive that demand, there can be no such
thing.

JULY 24, 1996

I was thinking today of the beatings my mother used to give me. I came to enjoy them very early on, and to take them silently, adoringly. Since then I have come to equate silence with extreme pleasure. But that silence was never silence, really. It was a kind of awful familiar music piped in from nowhere at the least possible volume. Like here, today.

July 27, 1996

So many drive-through people. Of course, there is really no such thing as driving *through*—one drives *by*. And who would drive by a Wendy's? Who would be so ridiculous as to assume that he could simply *extract* what he needs from a visit without actually making the visit, without standing awhile inside the blessed delusion of a manned source? How fast the dead have learned to bury the dead.

JULY 28, 1996

One of my favorite moments is when a woman bends down and unbuttons and unzips a man's pants; there is such a feeling of providence somehow. I can't help but feel that she has come, in this moment, to know the uselessness of words, and come, too, into a casual affirmation of the life that is inside words but has no power to use them. One yearns for such affirmation, or at least a view on to it.

JULY 29, 1996

I sort of recognize your employees, but not so much as you'd think. I believe they recognize me. When I think about it, the faces that really stay etched in my mind are the faces of porn stars. Only in porn, it seems, does a face acquire the peculiar glow of its ownmost rhythmic ambiguity. It's sad to everyday come to Wendy's and see faces that will never be given to me in their full porn depth.

JULY 30, 1996

So much anal bleeding. I worry sometimes. I wish Wendy's had a mascot community; mascots can be used to deal with these kind of worries. You could have a Professor Steak Sandwich, who is both a steak sandwich and a rectal bleeder, and he could interact with the other mascots in ways that entertain, inform, and reassure us about rectal health and being at Wendy's.

July 31, 1996

Your employees are beautiful—they do not have authority.
Even the manager has no authority—if pushed, he will
just call someone, who also has no ultimate authority. It's
extremely pleasing to recognize this fact—one feels so fairly
situated in the teeming absence of authors. At Wendy's, one
writes not from an author, but *to* an author, a sleeping
owner who will never wake.

AUGUST 1, 1996

First I have to thank the Lord Jesus Christ. It is only through Him that I am able to order anything at all, let alone eat it. It is only through Him, through His gift to me, that I am able to move my eyeballs from left to right, right to left, and to crane my neck the way I do. Imagine trying to live without being able to move your eyeballs or crane your neck! Imagine never being blessed with teeth, tongue, or tingle!

AUGUST 2, 1996

There is the question of who I really am, the tiger or the trainer. Am I this caged pulse, this pacing strength and silence, or do I stand around it, calming it, endlessly talking, singing, making whatever noise I can to bring it closer to sleep? Clearly I am the trainer. But there are moments when I put myself to sleep, and then only the tiger is, and there is nothing to be afraid of.

AUGUST 3, 1996

I love each distinct moment of my visit, but I love each so much and the love so much coheres that I am compelled to wish I could feel it all at once—one *thwack* across the mind. If I had my way, my life would be a happy succession of such thwacks, and I'd be the tight reeling that comes just after and begins slowly to lose itself, and to crave another good maker. But I can't even get one good thwack.

AUGUST 5, 1996

Everything comes to those who wait. Everything comes to those who don't wait, too. Everything comes—I guess that's the point. What to do, considering? I like to eat the flesh of certain animals three times each day and to lick the flesh of my own animal. It seems callous to say so, but then saying in itself is a kind of sudden ignorance of where everything is coming.

AUGUST 7, 1996

When my head hurts I don't need a doctor to tell me why;
I know it's because there's nowhere to put it. Where it's put
dissolves, and then there is my head, scorching, freezing,
dripping against a simple insistence on temporary limits.
Today was just so. I felt such revulsion looking at my fries,
each one exposed so much like myself, but even needier,
trusting me, my head, belly, for shelter. There's no shelter
here, friends.

AUGUST 8, 1996

Foucault says knowledge wasn't made for understanding but for cutting. For the Wendy's worker, that's especially true. The Wendy's worker *knows*—he does not understand—and his knowledge is alive with results. It is only for *us* to understand. In understanding, we construct, justify, and secure ourselves *above work*. This is how we conceal the knives and restrict their use to the production of delicious results.

AUGUST 10, 1996

What about an item that tastes good but also causes pain —
you could call them Painin' Cakes. Certain sharp pains,
especially shooting pains in the chest or abdomen, are rare,
and the experience is made faint by anxiety — that is, not
knowing whether or not extinction is near. If one knew that
the pains were not serious, one could enjoy them more, and
better learn one's lesson.

AUGUST 11, 1996

I would be so happy to be just a doctor. What a thought that is! But I am an over-doctor, a doctor of the doctor, or worse, an over-over-doctor... and each stage in the remove (retreat?) is no more successful than the last. Indeed, each patient—*my self* just a day ago—dies. I go on, barely a doctor now, even if my first patient, the exception, the one I abandoned and never was, struggles somehow on.

AUGUST 12, 1996

The fact of your burgers. I grasp it in some sense. I suppose this is knowledge. Abstracted from the meal, it fades. Then again, it's too brilliant to be much discerned during the meal. Knowledge is strongest during digestion, the effortless incomprehensible re-incorporation of the fact. I have knowledge, then—never information. Information is evidence of an anorexic among us.

August 13, 1996

Today I've been saying "schunk" every time I perform a small task. When I close the refrigerator door, for example, or put an ice-cube in my glass of Jim Beam. There are acts, though, that "schunk" cannot adequately bear witness to. For instance, this morning at breakfast I watched a video where several men came all at once in a woman's face: *sheer* schunklessness.

AUGUST 15, 1996

The incumbent faces never win. And they campaign so hard. The first-time faces, the faces that win, don't campaign at all. It doesn't seem fair. All day everyday all there is is the campaign of the incumbent faces. It's so depressing, listening to them and knowing they won't win. Worst of all is the concession speech, wherein the first-time faces are suddenly, out of politeness, deemed worthy of office.

AUGUST 16, 1996

My penis, it sounds like confetti. My face is too strong, so forget it. My sleep is burning, so let it. There's just so much to prove since I've come. Too much to prove all alone. Too much to prove since I've come. Too much to prove all alone. And time, time rolls on like a mountain—oh, there's just so much to prove. And I just can't prove it's undue.

AUGUST 17, 1996

There was a sort of long line today. As I stood there in it among my species, I kept repeating: "I have no constancy, I have no constancy." My species seemed to think that I was wrong, and seemed angry at me for being wrong in public. They are so easily frustrated by the truth. And the truth, for them, is just that ordinary awful time in which they have to wait to make an order.

AUGUST 18, 1996

We've become a *throw-away* society! they gasp. Well, could this be because we've discovered, *finally*, that we're a throw-away organism… living in a throw-away land? I think it's just this discovery that's prompted so much righteous organization against "waste." I'm happy to every day get a brand new ornate yellow cup, drink half my Coke, then abandon the thing altogether and forever.

AUGUST 19, 1996

Today I was thinking that it might be nice to be able, in one's last days, to move into a Wendy's. Perhaps a Wendy's life-support system could even be created and given a Wendy's slant; liquid fries, for instance, and burgers and Frosties continually dripped into one's vegetable dream locus. It would intensify the visits of the well, too, to see that such a care is being taken for their destiny.

August 20, 1996

This morning before my visit I drank more coffee than ever before. I went way out past hunger, my heart racing, missing beats. When I got to Wendy's I was beginning to crash and I had the great urge to go and sit down with an old couple and convince them to take me—to immerse me in the muted routine that springs from their basest assumption and hides the simple fact of their faces running out on them.

AUGUST 21, 1996

It is important to be no one. To be *someone*—isn't that like being one of those candles that's shaped like a lion, or an altar boy? For a candle, how strange it is to worry over keeping a distinct shape? I see so many of these worriers— blind twisted forms melting under their tiny flames. My flame is huge; at the tedious party of Relative Difference, no one wants to sit near me.

August 22, 1996

There used to be a little Ma-and-Pa restaurant across the road, but it couldn't keep up. Everyone over there acted all familiar and cozy, like they knew exactly where they were. Like they were *natives*. Natives!! *Execute the natives,* insofar as they claim to be! Build Wendy's everywhere and all alike—and do not fear: you cannot, you CAN NOT ever step into the same Wendy's twice.

August 25, 1996

I see various very strange people in Wendy's—the strangest of all being, clearly, the *serious Christians*. Usually strangeness is a pleasure to behold, but in this case I confess that I feel only a kind of empty horror. People *eating* toward eternity! People *looking nice* toward eternity! It is terrible to be real, I know, but it is more terrible to be *long*.

AUGUST 26, 1996

Very high on marijuana brownies, I could not speak today at the register. I kept stepping aside for other customers and staring hard at the menu. I was overwhelmed by the chicken sandwich pictured there, but had no words for it. I kept saying, *"there,* that one... the man dressed like a woman." It's hard to get served when one understands the signifier as a process.

AUGUST 27, 1996

Still high on those brownies, but coming down. I've eaten, in the past twenty-four hours, so very many burgers and chicken sandwiches. The Sea of Coke is heavy today with meat—its cold swells with the meaty goodness that objects to language. Some kids drift by, talking. One of them says, "that sucks dead donkey dicks," and the other agrees. Imagine.

AUGUST 28, 1996

Moving my bowels at home I feel a great recognition
arising: *good old me*. Today I had to shit at Wendy's. As I
let it go, I felt zero recognition—the *good old me* was
nowhere to be found. To my surprise, I felt somewhat
relieved, even joyful, to sense anew the careful absence of
where I've come from. To be alive is to shit into a strange
place.

AUGUST 31, 1996

Wendy is possessed of—or possessed by—a barbaric coquettishness. She bodies forth that space wherein these two terms cannot be co-extensive, where one must *give* and become the other. Wendy is just this impossible space, this holding close of forces which seek to part, to come into themselves. Wendy lets neither come fully into itself; she allows no essence but her own.

SEPTEMBER 2, 1996

I love the cleanliness of a Wendy's. Such a clean is not in
any sense a banishing of genitalia; it is the creation of a
quiet bright mind-space that allows for the deliciousness of
genitalia to become obvious. I look out over the colorful
clean tables and the pretty food posters and *I like people*
again; each has a dick and balls, or a cunt and titties, which,
clean, are simply enjoyable.

SEPTEMBER 3, 1996

There may be no you—no other to receive and understand these revelations of myself. The Post Office may burn them for all I know. It's not important. I only need you as a good idea—to make me apparent. I love you, even if you don't understand me, even if you burn my attempts to reach you, even if you are no one, nowhere. After all, I warm my hands by the same fires.

September 5, 1996

Naturally I think about smashing the skulls and the rib-
cages of the other customers. They stand in line so smug—
like they were safe, *outside* the desires of or for an other.
It's as if, for them, there is no *other*'s desire—as if desire was
one thing, and was *ours*. Restraining myself is not *dishonest*.
It's a way of maintaining a keen sense of the unforeseeable
injuries which shall reunite us.

SEPTEMBER 6, 1996

I'm a cute little puppy in a Pound. Sometimes other customers are like people wandering through and not choosing me. Other times they're like Pound employees, just getting done what they need to get done. Sometimes I think, *Which one of you will take me home and train me to be good.* Sometimes I think, *Which one of you will put me to sleep.*

SEPTEMBER 7, 1996

I rarely ask anything of you because I'm a realist. There is something, though, I'd like to ask. You know the little spot of lawn outside—the immaculate green rectangle between the sidewalk and the parking lot. I'd like it if you put a baited tiger-trap there. It would show just how far we've come in the meat industry and it would make clear precisely how much *time* we now save (and then waste) every day.

SEPTEMBER 8, 1996

At bottom, they say: get *more* out of life. *More what?* If it's just more meat, more Coke, more sex, more images, *more* of everything... then the idea makes no sense. Or rather, it makes too much sense, neurotically overloading us with it. Sense is the ultimate event for us talkers, I know, but we're vivid there in it only when its brutality is humble, unencumbered, and free of greedy systems.

September 10, 1996

I wanted to say today to my register-person that my penis was broad. "My dick is broad," I would say, or "Do you understand how *broad* my cock is?" Maybe simply, "The breadth of my penis." What's the point? There are times when ambiguity is not a failure to tend to a specific concern, but rather, is an articulation of *the limits* of concern, without which we are certainly nobody.

SEPTEMBER 11, 1996

Glottal thrust supersedes nascent envy, but who really gives
a good goddamn? There is no blood-light, blood-voice,
blood-ring, despite all my insisting. Anti-polar dementia
sweeps up the sublimated vestiges of the sheer. Pony, pony,
pony—all night long. How could you do this to me? How
could you! Didn't I sleep, didn't I weep beside you?

SEPTEMBER 12, 1996

I seek respite from tolerance, in every sense. Stop giving me what I want! Say to me, "This has gone far enough!" Put me under arrest, take me to the other side of the register! Take me back into the manager's tiny office and explain to me the gross error of my design! Manage me! To manage—what is that? *To not let be.*

SEPTEMBER 13, 1996

Rather than restrict sexual activity to a specific set of acts, or restrict the articulation of such acts, we need only draw real lines, lines upon the earth, to mark *whether or not* sexuality is in this place active. The question is: *is sex now, here?* If it is, well then. If it isn't, as, in Wendy's, it always isn't, then a campaign dawns, and we stand fast in the sexy inception of already failed propaganda.

SEPTEMBER 14, 1996

Last night I dreamt that I pissed on Wendy's head. I entered
the restroom, approached the urinal, and started pissing,
when suddenly I realized it was not a urinal at all... but
Wendy. As I began to protest (to the dream itself) I
understood that I *must have* known it was her. I felt
ashamed, yet wronged. I also felt like the only thing that
I ever wanted to happen was finally happening.

SEPTEMBER 16, 1996

Today I walked in and they wrapped me in meat. They stitched the meat to me with empty sentences. They smeared the stitches with faces—I don't know whose. They wrapped it all up in my voice, but this never really worked. When I spoke you could only hear the faces smeared into stitches the color of meat. So I began, without confidence, to try to take off my voice.

September 18, 1996

I don't think Wendy's coffee has such a good taste. This is
not to say I don't like it. I like it very much. Its poor taste
keeps my intentions clear; I drink coffee for the enthusiasm-
prod, not for the taste. The taste, when it is too pleasant,
can distract one from what matters most—the deep writhing
jolt. Of course, some taste is necessary so that the jolt
seems, at bottom, inadvertent.

SEPTEMBER 19, 1996

Some guy pushing a petition, a meeting. "You don't know me," I said. "I'm an avowed spectator." "Well, just come down and watch," he said. "That's just it," I said. "You people aren't satisfied watching—you want to *be* the show, and to make this happen you're willing to give up the only thing in the world of any value: *free time*." In his mind, I could sense the word "evil" forming.

September 20, 1996

Today I had a Biggie. Usually I just have a small, and refill. Why pay more? But today I needed a Biggie inside me. Some days, I guess, are like that. Only a Biggie will do. You wake up and you know: today I will get a Biggie and I will put it inside me and I will feel better. One time I saw a guy with three Biggies at once. One wonders not about him but about what it is that holds us back.

SEPTEMBER 21, 1996

If I had to say what Wendy really was—if she had to be one thing instead of a field of various energies—I think I'd have to say that she was a penis. Something about her face and the shape of her hair, the muffled red coherence of head and torso, and perhaps too her lack of arms and legs. A penis is founded in just such a lack of limbs; it's really amazing when it arrives anywhere.

SEPTEMBER 22, 1996

Wendy's will burn, Wendy's will jerk, Wendy's is open forever. Wendy, however, will never appear. Wendy will never speak or laugh—she will never give herself away. Wendy will never sit upon my knee, or your knee, or the knee of any living organism. Wendy will restrain herself in almost every fashion. Wendy's will burn, Wendy's will jerk, Wendy's is open forever.

SEPTEMBER 23, 1996

Gangbang weather for the first time in weeks. Makes me want to behave. Just go out and behave in the stinky sunlight. In my biography, they'll say that I never behaved at all, and that the sunlight was no stinkier than usual. But that is the business of biography; biography is the dream of a misbehavior that is able not only to endure the stinky sunlight, but to forget it. Its incalculable insistence.

SEPTEMBER 24, 1996

I love to watch a dick slamming in and out of a cunt or an asshole. The only way t.v. could enhance Wendy's is if it was confined to showing non-stop hardcore pornography without sound. No ridiculous assertion of plot or personality. Just the real pleasure of lacking language. Just a reassuring view of the signifier itself as it finds its way to its ancient hiding place in broad daylight.

SEPTEMBER 25, 1996

A woman with twins today, aged five or six. Almost perfect replicas. They sit eating, staring off now and then into the mid-air realm, the not-eating realm. They stare out knowing that their mother is there. They stare out from the good of eating. I want to ask them: *is that good already not good enough? And do you understand already that there is something more original than a mother?*

SEPTEMBER 27, 1996

If we think of the future as The Pritty Titty Bah-B-Q, and the past as A Motion Excreting Machine (excreting through the pores), we get a much clearer picture of the present. While the present is forever beginning to be a buffet, it is always already eaten away to the point of shimmering. This shimmering should not be confused with what is actually edible.

SEPTEMBER 29, 1996

If I had two dwarves who followed me about and inquired endlessly into my philosophy, I'd want them to be named Munley and Leffage. And I'd say to them, "Munley, Leffage, I have no philosophy, or none I'd want anyone else to know about. Why would I want anyone else to know my philosophy—I'm no Emperor, and my life is not something which should ever be repeated."

September 30, 1996

I don't like the idea of "old fashioned" hamburgers. The desire to dwell in *the ways of old* reduces being to tourism. It puts a "Ye Olde" in front of every location. Ye Olde Drugstore, Ye Olde Restroom, Ye Olde Prison, Ye Olde Strip Club, Ye Olde Convenience Store. The only place that still is a place—and Wendy's is, despite this silly slogan—exists primarily *before*, not after, history.

OCTOBER 2, 1996

To take someone's buttocks in your hands, one cheek in each hand—is there any greater earthly event? And yet, I've never heard someone say so. To say so seems to threaten the very core of so-called humanity. That is, to say so undermines the abstraction—the *bodiless* image—with which "human" identity proposes it is moving forward toward... toward... toward what?

OCTOBER 5, 1996

Wendy is not pussel-gutted—that's what I mean. She's the mid-air creature we used to call a god and now can't take seriously. The mid-air untouched by pussel-gut lack of destiny. We, pussel-gutted, resound in the tangled shameful thrust of borrowing pronouns we can't repay. We, a teeming heap of real, and she, the young pretty Never it pretends to, every chance it gets.

OCTOBER 7, 1996

Why is there somewhere that is not Wendy's? The question haunts me. Perhaps there need be *a coming into* Wendy's, a coming into that's only possible when there is a not-Wendy's. Perhaps the question should be: *is there* truly somewhere that is not Wendy's? Could our conception of where we are have developed within an unconscious need to forget how far Wendy's truly extends?

OCTOBER 8, 1996

It would bring me to despair to think that I could get a Frosty in my own kitchen. I need believe that a Frosty can only be gotten *outside* of where I ordinarily dwell. *To be constantly* in the place of real Frosties—this is unthinkable, somehow unbearable. The fact is: to be a subject of language is to desire an Event, and an Event needs a nothing to move out of, to seem to begin.

OCTOBER 9, 1996

I sometimes think of working at Wendy's. It would be so fine, so glamorous. To fulfill so many pressing, wanton needs in such a short period of time—I don't know that it wouldn't go to my head. I think I have so far resisted the idea for this reason. Also, I have always suspected that, glamour aside, it is better to be served than to serve, better to give than to receive orders.

OCTOBER 10, 1996

Today I've been saying "schink" instead of "schunk" as I perform the small events of my persistence. "Schink" is more precise than "schunk," indicating a narrower, shallower act. Closing the refrigerator—*schink*—dropping ice-cubes in my glass of Jim Beam—*schink, schink*. It is a tidier existence, as though *things* were readier to be spoken of. The erosion of the soul is endless.

OCTOBER 11, 1996

Each day I walk to Wendy's. As I approach, especially crossing the parking lot, I begin to feel powerfully *ordinary*. I feel like I am who I have always been, and like I'm going somewhere to stay. I feel all stories returning to myth—a dense forest returning to a bed of bright seeds. As I assert my order, the most routine routine in the world hides me in its wake, as mysteriously *fitting* as a midget's big penis.

OCTOBER 12, 1996

Like a man who out of anger explodes into a sound he will
never know the meaning of, that he will never even hear
but will only know in the awkward effects of its being
heard—and who then finds himself suddenly in the
absence of that sound, having resumed himself as if he
could not possibly have contained its violence, its
inarticulate force, I come to stand on the other side of my
order.

OCTOBER 15, 1996

Like a bowl of fresh fruit suddenly alone in the Arctic night, like a killer under arrest for an unrelated misdemeanor, like a flightless bird thrown up into the air by a cruel child, like an abandoned car in the middle of a huge, empty parking lot, like a juggler dreaming of being tied down, like a young priest watching porn in the early morning, I sit in my booth and decide nothing.

OCTOBER 16, 1996

As with most things, writing to you is something I do without any explicit justification. Are my visits insufficient? The ordering, the eating and the drinking—are these not enough? I don't know. I think my visits are, if not sufficient, at least *pleasing*, and maybe writing is just an effort to loiter there, to allow that pleasure to resonate, and to imply the endlessly forgotten source.

OCTOBER 17, 1996

Wendy is not a girl—she is a sign. This means she does not have appendages or orifices—she is herself, at once, an appendage *and* an orifice. As a sign, she holds within herself—radiantly implicit—that orifice which language must have always already have penetrated, just as she holds into view the penetrating appendage. She is a girl only in the mind of the customer, the lonely hermaphroditic homestead of significance.

October 18, 1996

For no reason, no event, do I persist, echo. I persist, echo, only in order *not to*, and *not to*, and *not to*. I am a defense — altogether a defense — and a defense employed by I know not who. Sometimes, my meal finished, I sit in my booth and wonder: what am I defending? And I can only answer: I am defending whatever it is that I am devouring.

OCTOBER 19, 1996

Big hole, little hole, eatin' hole, plow. You didn't eat me because I'm not now. Big hole, little hole, shittin' hole, plow. You didn't eat me because I'm not now. Big hole, little hole, dyin' hole, plow. You didn't know me, you didn't know how. Big hole, little hole, speakin' hole, wow! You didn't come here, you were the plow.

OCTOBER 21, 1996

There's so little I have to tell you—how can I even begin?
There aren't few enough words to say what I have to say. I
sense, though, that you—you in an office somewhere, you
in a place without hunger, a place which only vaguely, only
technically, stands for another place—you know how I feel.
I like to think that you have even come here yourself, after
work, to where there is so little to say. Where there is
sustenance.

OCTOBER 22, 1996

So much pleasure in drug ritual, so little pleasure in all else. To come to one's senses—to let the mind *clench*—and lo, the myriad abstract guardians of the clenching have already arisen and taken their positions! You, WORKER, you exist to guard the streets that lead to Wendy's coffee, Wendy's Coke, Wendy's assorted meats. The war against drugs is a war against you, against the good sense that, daily, discards destiny.

OCTOBER 23, 1996

I've come gradually, in these missives, into a kind of discomfort. I've come to feel that *I should be writing*, even when I've already written. The more I write, the more I feel *I haven't written*. This *lacking writing* presses on me. After a meal, there was once a great bland pleasure, a lewd laughing repetition of location. Now I am afraid to laugh, afraid to repeat myself, as though something new, something better, needed to be said.

OCTOBER 25, 1996

No race, no gene pool, is inferior to another, and slavery should not be organized that way. Racial slavery inevitably makes countless mistakes. Also, slavery should never be cruel—cruelty is a sign of its demise. Basically, slavery is just the voice of the master, and it only ever says: *here is your work.* The end of slavery is just the end of work, the ridiculous first step of an impossible exodus. Let it commence.

OCTOBER 28, 1996

I think you need pain-killers on the menu. It is the next step in "civilization." The present is so full of pain, and it is where we keep finding ourselves. Don't tell me I want to *run away* from the present—nothing could be further from the truth. When I am *without* pain-killers—that is when I hide, that is when I run away. It is my desire to run *into* the present; what I want is for the collision to be more decisive.

OCTOBER 29, 1996

Sometimes there's no coffee in the coffee. I plow through it and it is definitely a *coffee area*, but there's no coffee in it. I always think they'll be a little at the bottom of the cup, but there never is. If it's missing at all, it's all missing. The fact is, coffee isn't just a substance—it's an event, and its manifestation depends on countless subtle conditions, most of which are not speakable.

OCTOBER 31, 1996

Urine time again. Later, maybe cheap moan-lodging with
countless vacancies. Of course, blunt costumes include
themselves. Who arrives in splinters and undresses the
brain-dead grooms? Who withdraws like animal sound?
Hungle-popping butt-dress. Who hides like a book in the
sauce? The sauce which doesn't work. The book which
sells. What did I tell you?

NOVEMBER 2, 1996

Bits of Wendy-flags flutter sadly in the rainy wind. It's so dark. To eat today feels like a shocking rudeness—one continually burns with shame but cannot understand why. It's as though our whole intention was suddenly terribly misguided, as though the site we built on turned out to be swamp, or someone else's property. And, as in a dream, there is no moment after finding out.

NOVEMBER 3, 1996

Surgeon-light booming. I take a bite. This recent organization of animals, chunks of homelessness dwindling. I take a sip. Gusts of patience—nothing to worry about. I take a bite. Grass finding always a new naive cause. I take a bite. Surgeon-light booming—nothing to worry about. I take a sip. Loud shadow of animals in the causeway, home-gouging. I take a sip, a bite. Guts of patients.

November 8, 1996

It seems to me your work force is quite meaningfully divided. The register workers, I feel, are Cowboys, whereas the kitchen workers are Indians. Why conceal this? Why not let them dress in the way they are naturally inclined to dress? Do you fear it would bring back too many bad memories—undermine cooperation? Do you have that little faith in the dignity of the task from which their present cooperation stems?

NOVEMBER 9, 1996

To have dominated nothing, that is my real claim. It gets
lost among the countless other claims I make to survive. Its
getting lost is the only happiness I know. When it gets lost,
really lost, I am again a true reservoir, and again the nothing
can fill me up to overflowing. A burger is nothing. A Coke
is nothing. A Frosty is nothing. I have dominated nothing.

November 10, 1996

The thought-cake stream is only visible at night. Big white cakes moving slow, one after the other, into oblivion. These cakes aren't to be eaten. They're just for show, as though the night needed their senseless procession to remain its own dark self. One night you will wade out, when the hunger becomes too much, and you will taste this cake, and you will know, then, for certain, that it was only for show.

NOVEMBER 11, 1996

Can you not feel Wendy's blindness, her exile, as she looks down at you from the sign? What terrible thing has she done to deserve exile in such a barren place? *She, like Oedipus, was a child.* Surviving infancy is the true Oedipal crime, and the Wendy's sign encompasses the whole of this drama, illuminating the crime—*the child*—with its endless eye-bursting punishment, *the sign.*

NOVEMBER 12, 1996

I'd like to have photos of your employees for my home. So many move on without warning and I'm left with just a few memories. One boy who was afraid to look at me as he took my order. A young woman who seem dazed, distant, as she handed me a mustard pack. I will forget these things, but I'd like to forget them more slowly, more surely.

November 13, 1996

As hypotheticals go, "man" seems to me the most damaging.
By damage I mean the vagueness it causes to accrue upon
the really rather specific avenues we go down. I think
"creature" is a much less damaging term to live under; a
creature is always implicitly conjured, somehow unfit for its
own country, and so, apt to transform itself, if not evolve.

November 14, 1996

Today the restaurant was filled with warmth, a spirit of caring. The food was just right and the service was prompt. For the first time this season, snow began to fall. Parents laughed with their children. Handsome employees made witty—but not inconsiderate—remarks. Retired couples were given Extra Value coupons. I felt like getting fucked up and watching t.v. forever.

NOVEMBER 15, 1996

A beautiful woman with a Biggie. Nothing else—just a Biggie. She sat alone; she seemed like she was waiting for someone. What lucky soul could make a beautiful woman with a Biggie wait? Who has that kind of power? What person would a beautiful woman with a Biggie find attractive? Only one answer made sense to me: *another beautiful woman with a Biggie.*

NOVEMBER 16, 1996

It's good, this not knowing anyone's name. The employees have name-tags, but no one believes them. Their anonymity is far too obvious. How monstrous to introduce oneself to one's register person! How useless, how wearying, that information is! Only the shouted names of children make sense here, denoting not a person but a drifting off, a subversive fascination.

NOVEMBER 17, 1996

I eavesdrop on people at Wendy's. I notice they never talk
about their assholes. It's not that I think an asshole, as an
abstract (as Platonic form if you will), is so interesting. It's
specific assholes that are interesting—my asshole as
compared with Nick's, yours as compared with Ted's or
Mary's. How one experiences another's asshole speaks
volumes—it seems selfish not to make these volumes
readily available.

NOVEMBER 18, 1996

I am always trying to take a harem by force. At Wendy's this effort subsides and is transformed. What is the new effort? It is an effort *not to be famous*. This effort begins with recognition of my fame, which, as it turns out, is only my failure to be comfortable as a mute orator. The new effort differs most obviously from my own in that it begins to succeed.

NOVEMBER 19, 1996

Some tentative destinics plague us. One of the least degrading is the one with baths. Wendy's could go that way, become a bath-place. It certainly isn't the worst idea. Instead of booths and tables, there would be hot-tubs. The tubs would afford more opportunity for ogling (righteous vision). Of course, there is the danger of delirium, *loitering*, disrespecting the real distances hunger has birthed and should never abandon.

NOVEMBER 20, 1996

I feel like I have nothing to tell you today. It's not that I think you already understand what I feel, and it's not that I think "everything's already been said." It's more like the feelings themselves are resentful toward the idea of their being made public—like they have a humility that makes them cringe at the thought of a witness. I believe it is at this point that one tends to say, "I feel fine."

November 21, 1996

Imagine being a man's wife for twenty years and then finding out that he pees sitting down. A like moment, I fear, awaits me. I come to Wendy's because I know such a moment can't happen here. I know, too, that I can't stay. My refuge, then, is like an argument that only ever begins because it can't believe what it knows. After awhile, it only goes on for the sound of its voice—that sound which, miraculously, briefly, resists curiosity.

NOVEMBER 22, 1996

If we are to believe what modern science has to tell us, we should really relax. That is, we are a sea, not a tenant farmer. Wendy's, while quite actively participating in the tenant farming structure, takes pains to conceal its participation. This is not a deceit. It is way of demonstrating that the sea, so long as it rises up against the tenant farming structure, is incapable of relaxing.

NOVEMBER 25, 1996

This idiotic notion that one should love the other customers. Love here really only means: *agree, for the time being, not to attack*. People pretend, though, that each customer is an irreplaceable piece of some priceless puzzle—like the death of each customer is significant for every other customer. It's just not true; one cannot love what one does not know, and—fortunately—one knows very little.

NOVEMBER 26, 1996

Artaud prefigures the experience of being on speed while standing under a Wendy's menu when he writes: "In it we feel a grinding of sluices, a kind of horrible volcanic shock from which the light of day has been *dissociated*. And from this clash, from the tearing of two principles, all potential images are born in a thrust stronger than a ground swell."

NOVEMBER 27, 1996

The Virgin Mother appeared to me today. She was holding two baked potatoes with sour cream and chives. "They're delicious," she said, and she smiled, emanating a great white light. I took one from her. It was warm and inviting. I cut into it with my plastic fork and plastic knife and I took a bite. It was, as usual, very dry. She held out the other potato to me. "You try it," I said, "it's dry as fuck."

November 28, 1996

If I had a dog I would want to call it either "Chicken" or "The Chicken." I would never call my dog "A Chicken," and I wouldn't spend time with anyone who could. I think most dogs incline one to call them Chicken, but there are certainly a few who make the definite article seem fitting, if not necessary. The best thing, though, is not to have a dog.

DECEMBER 1, 1996

Open oodles of olden operation. Opaque oracle-object.
Oafish obeisance. Otiose ornament, ordering outlandish
ought. Ornery oblation of optic ordeal. Open oodles of
olden obeisance. Oafish outland oracle-object. Otiose
ought operation. Ornament ouster. Otiose outland oodles.
Ought-object ouster. Open oodles of oafishness. Open
oodles of otiose outland.

DECEMBER 3, 1996

Today I had fifteen dollars worth of coffees. I got them one at a time, and dined in. The first five were leisurely, but then the leisure disintegrated. I went through the last five in about five minutes. After awhile the register girl looked at her manager as if to say: "Is there something we should do?" The manager said nothing. I said nothing. We understood one another perfectly.

DECEMBER 6, 1996

I've done what you wanted, now you must let me go. You
promised that if I lived up to my part of the bargain I could
go free. It doesn't matter that the thing didn't work out—
that was not my fault. The deal was: I do my part, I get my
freedom, no matter what. You know and I know that if you
don't honor your word, there's nothing I can do. Nothing,
that is, except *hate you* with all my heart.

December 7, 1996 (Pearl Harbor Day)

Let's say they could move all the stones into place. And they could move the stories over on to writhing armies of light sleep. And let's say, too, that they could organize all the family albums so that we could see exactly who gestured to who and how the gestures were taken. Say they could even move the sea-bottom into vacant lots. With all this done, they'd be no less determined by a little slap and tickle.

DECEMBER 8, 1996

To stroke another customer's head. Run my fingers through his hair and whisper to him: "you're going to be *all right*...." I would be called *responsible* for doing all of this if he was bleeding to death on the floor, but I would be called *inappropriate* if I did it when he was in good health. I would be, like all trustworthy prophets, called a nuisance and promptly arrested.

DECEMBER 10, 1996

Ideas protrude. They are less false than what they protrude into—the so-called "nature." They're less false only because they're *hauled*, and the hauler can still be suspicioned in their protruding. There is no actual hauler, of course, but in his absence we can nevertheless feel the way the gigantic bed keeps itself clean. When it's really clean it writes upon itself: *I'm going to let you die.*

DECEMBER 11, 1996

Thinking presses on one, demands that *being* admit its foundation in sense. *Faith* relieves this pressure. Its strange babbling is learned intuitively, like a way of laughing. The most stupefying faith there has ever been is the faith in "heaven." Such a faith proposes the abrupt and complete end of sense. This proposal *cannot even conceivably* be accepted, however much one cries, "I accept, I accept."

DECEMBER 12, 1996

During a heart transplant the body is packed in ice to keep it from damage while the defective heart is removed and the new heart is not yet in place. This body is a fine way to describe my spirit. The "I" has been removed. All that depends upon the "I," however, somehow persists. Such a persistence can't last, but can't be helped. The "I" itself can't last—that's why it was removed in the first place.

DECEMBER 14, 1996

I always feel like someone at Wendy's is going to *help me change*. It's so hard to really change—most of the time I don't even think of it as a possibility. At Wendy's, though, especially when I've ordered and I know that good people are working hard to bring me what I deserve, I know I *can* change. I can become something truly special, like an escaped death-row inmate or a twelve-year-old prostitute.

DECEMBER 15, 1996

When I sit down on a cold toilet seat at home I make a little sound to distract myself from the feeling of cold on my ass. At Wendy's I cannot make the sound. Well, that isn't quite true—I still make the sound *in my mind*. Can it be called a sound, though, if it has no sound? How is it that a sound persists—intact—without its real self? This stubborn drifting away from the real is the dumb impulse of all speakers.

DECEMBER 16, 1996

Uncalled-for boy-sounds strum the bloody tits. The feathers fall out of the birds. The birds fall out of the trees. The trees fall out of the ground. There is no sound. There is no lost and found. The bloody tits lack a symbol. The boy-sounds strum the lack. There is no sound. The birds fall back into the fallen trees. The feathers fall back into the birds. Wendy's is hiring.

DECEMBER 17, 1996

The factory pulls its sleepy lovers into a dirty "area." Sleep-aids are manufactured. Sleep almost comes to those who can afford it. The pornographer decides what to do. The "actors" say they understand. Big lights are hauled in and arranged around a couch. The couch is not special. The actors are not acting. The factory feels betrayed, steps up production. The actors can almost sleep now.

DECEMBER 18, 1996

To diverge from the expectable in choosing the central item would further distinguish Wendy's from competing realms. Perhaps a central item which was medicinal, in addition to being tasty, would depart radically enough: a mild cheddar anti-depressant shake, maybe. The easy distinction we make between food and medicine is fast evaporating; whosoever leaps in to this evaporation shall inherit the world.

DECEMBER 20, 1996

How nice it would be to have lived during a massive war effort. Things today are still massive, of course, and still a war effort, but something's different. Somehow the two are no longer intimate. The massive has many partners now, and the war effort seems to want to hide itself away, so as not to see the affairs of the massive. One hopes for a reconciliation but knows better.

DECEMBER 21, 1996

Insofar as one breathes, one stands inside the tedious pleasure of a guarded tumult. Such guards cannot but sicken, bore, and wander off. It is amazing how slowly the guards lose interest; inexplicable regret does not grow easily. As the guards wander off, though, it is fully grown, and the tumult, without fail, is exposed to writing, and, ultimately, even to being left alone.

DECEMBER 22, 1996

I drink tea at home but would never at Wendy's. Tea lacks
the necessary brutality. Tea pretends knowledge is
cumulative, a saturation. Coffee knows knowledge is an
endless betrayal-process, endlessly knocking the wind out
of *what I thought*. Coffee confuses and intertwines, for a
long moment, the immense strength of my betrayer with
my own small strength: steady impatience.

December 24, 1996 (Christmas Eve)

If we must put people to death, why not at Wendy's. Is midnight in a prison basement better? Wendy's provides the two things an execution needs most: plenty of light, and refreshments. The light allows the condemned to feel death as an inevitable blending. The refreshments allow the audience to take in their own hands the tamed substance and to feel themselves securely on this side of the blender.

December 25, 1996 (Christmas)

In a way, I collect pussies. I stream into the dull trace and sleep them off—sleep the pussies off. Then I start the collection over. It's easy, but it's so painful I sometimes have to lash out at inanimate objects. The pain is least when I can find someone else who has a collection and likes to talk. We discuss the pussies we've stolen and how we slept them off. The confession is endless.

DECEMBER 26, 1996

A sort of hell-garden would be useful. Often, after a meal, I feel inclined to lay myself out in the elements, as though dead, to be picked apart by birds and dogs. It is surprisingly difficult to find a suitable space. The garden I have in mind would be a simple concrete square right off the dining room, and would offer several boulders which one could drape oneself over and feel properly exposed.

DECEMBER 27, 1996

I can say without hesitation that if Wendy's ever started to "deliver" I would end my life. And in a way, my suicide would mimic Wendy's decision to "deliver." That is, I would decide that my blood, which, in my body, made sense, should flow out in to the dust, where it makes just more dust. *Our homes are dust?* you ask. Yes, our homes are dust. Don't pretend you are surprised.

DECEMBER 29, 1996

You know what I like. I like to arrive home and find everything missing—even the plastic cutlery. I like some dogs out back, looking. And we can settle in to the empty living room and speak our fatal disease. We will be so much in love!! Going for diagnosis together and coming back to the house to find everything missing. O God how warm the floor is on those nights! How beautiful your eyes!

DECEMBER 30, 1996

Why is it that, without the register, all Wendy's activity is halted? Ordering, eating, preparing the food—are we to believe all of this is subservient to the cash transaction? Marx wanted to take a sledge hammer to all registers. He hoped we'd recover our senses in the long lines that ensued. I don't think he understood how awful it is to actually climb over the counter.

DECEMBER 31, 1996 (NEW YEAR'S EVE)

Eschewing verse, I've assumed it best to break my lines like prose. I've assumed a visit a *full* thing—a thing demanding as many words as possible. But if it is indeed full, can I approach this fullness on such a small card? I've come to feel that my refusal to include silences, rather than reflecting the inherent *fullness* of a visit, more likely betrays my own anxious need to imply that fullness.

JANUARY 1, 1997 (NEW YEAR'S DAY)

Today a small child weeping. Perhaps weeping is the wrong
word. His mother explained to me that this was not true
grief—this was pretend grief. This was grief, she said,
designed to get something. And I thought, have I anything
but pretend grief? And I asked myself what I meant, in these
daily excretions of pretend grief, to acquire? And I couldn't
answer. And I felt true grief.

JANUARY 3, 1997

I've been sort of hesitant to mention this, but I believe that one of your employees—you *must* know the one I speak of—is a beaver. It's impossible to look into her face, to hear the sounds she makes, and to see the way she moves, the way she carries bits of wood, and to not feel that *this is a beaver*. I've not mentioned this before because, obviously, beavers are powerful creatures.

JANUARY 4, 1997

It's wonderful to think of meat sculpted to resemble a penis, but it's a different thing to actually have it on your plate. So long as it's just an idea, you can lick it, kiss it, in your mind, without feeling strange. When it's actually meat, though, one is suddenly unable, or unwilling, to carry out what one has been thinking. To actually bite it, even if it is just a dildo, seems monstrous.

JANUARY 5, 1997

come drain memory (during morning service) and dry-
hump the noisy shallows (busting in and drowned) in the
name of anyway-drillers (who know only this burial really)
eating away the way it sounds (in the Non) (in the pushed
area) (in the very front of the soldier-talk) knowing really
only busting in and feeding the approach of drowning in
the name:

JANUARY 7, 1997

What a joy it is to be alive! To wake late in the morning and have cups and cups and cups of coffee, and in the heightened blind pulse that follows to *play*, to *let language have its way*, to let the business of day *close down* with all of us still inside! We absolutely hang together in how dim the day gets. We hang by sentences. Listen! We hang by the sound of the shadow of a thread!

JANUARY 11, 1997

I love a lady's bottom. The family objects. The family says this love will mean the end of them. *What are they*, that this love could mean the end of them? A lady's bottom is as inevitable as it is lovable. Are we to conclude, then, that the universe is designed to threaten the family? Are we to believe that a lady's bottom is, in truth, a threat? In truth, the family is a threat, and love has cowered too long.

JANUARY 12, 1997

I don't think any of us would deny there are tufted
customers. We can certainly look the other way—or,
worse, we can pressure these customers to conceal their
tufts. We oscillate, I think, between these two strategies.
This oscillation should be understood as an impotency,
and used to actively locate the threshold of presence. That
we cannot survive this threshold is as irrelevant as the tufts
themselves.

JANUARY 14, 1997

I confess I don't feel like sending you my thoughts today.
I'd like to say that I have no thoughts, but that's not true.
I have no thoughts that seem worthy of clarification. Of
course, the distinction is ridiculous—NO thought is *worthy*
of clarification. Clarification is just the process the fantasy
needs to pretend it's on the way to itself. Fuck clarification;
give me the meat and leave me alone.

JANUARY 15, 1997

We're only getting dirtier! Dirtier and dirtier with every burger-bite, every Coke, every single fry. We are devices that need to be clean in order to function—in order to continue eating, to continue speaking—but we are increasingly incapable of cleaning ourselves! Listen to the devices struggle, caked with filth, to take another bite, speak another sentence. Listen to your heart!

JANUARY 16, 1997

Standing in Wendy's is like standing naked in your own
glass compartment in a room full of people similarly
compartmentalized. One is free to take in the nakedness
of others, if only from behind sturdy glass. It is possible to
communicate, but only within a crude signaling system that
makes conversation very limited. One must be satisfied with
this limitation, though: *one must not stare*.

JANUARY 17, 1997

We should not forget that we have arisen from a simple browsing hunger. Perhaps the next step, the *focused* browsing capability—farms leading to fast-food restaurants—isn't indicative of any real change. It doesn't solve hunger, after all. I'm comforted to think of Wendy's as a miraculous heap of meals, and to come to it every day like a vulture to a battlefield it could not have seen coming.

JANUARY 18, 1997

Why do we sit on the faces we love? I think it may be that we yearn to have our essence eaten away and we can only entrust this yearning to someone we love. The problem is that, as a face becomes loved, it ceases to be capable of the task. Could it be we truly yearn not for our essence to be eaten away, but for it to *seem* inedible? Why not sit on the faces of strangers otherwise?

January 19, 1997

These fucking teeny-bopper cunts—they'll steal your man as soon as look at you. Even if you don't have a man, they'll steal him. They'll steal him and they'll take him back to their fucking teeny-bopper bedroom. Then they'll suck his dick *real slow* as though they've never sucked a dick before and they'll say, "it's so big!" even if it isn't. And then afterwards they'll act like they never said it was big at all.

JANUARY 20, 1997

People often ask what my "opinion" is. Well, I guess my opinion is that the baked potatoes are too dry. Oh, but it isn't only that—that isn't all I mean! Why must I be torn apart like this? Why must we converse with one another in this fashion—this "opinion" exchange? Is there no alternative? Isn't it possible to restrict ourselves to the facts? Would that be so terrible?

JANUARY 23, 1997

I always expect to see Wendy's covered with Revolution banners. History is no longer possible, though, except as the history of advertisement. A cry of "Revolution" from Wendy's would be taken no differently than Taco Bell's cry of "Run For The Border!" Each is an attempt to generate hunger and to prefigure its outcome. Could revolution have ever been anything more?

JANUARY 25, 1997

Light is hectic. That's obvious, and it should tell us something. *Where we are* is inimical to us. We have overlooked the plain facts too long. How many times will we allow ourselves to be betrayed? It isn't as though *where we are* has given itself to us—we have taken it! Do not believe otherwise! A *home* should be like Wendy's: discreet, impersonal, practical, and altogether unholy.

JANUARY 26, 1997

I want our first time to be special. Candles, soft music, moonlight. I want everything to be just right. I don't want to feel rushed. I don't want the first time to be in some cheap motel. I want it to feel like it was completely meant to be. That way, when I suck your pussy, ease four fingers up your lubricated asshole, pinch your nipples and drench you in cum, it will be really beautiful.

JANUARY 27, 1997

There's no stink of death. There's just a warmish wacky-woo, a shining shimmy-shoo. Hunt the ice if it comes to that, my honorable Antarctic brethren. Let the sun make of this hole a wordy casket! We shall feast upon ice tonight in our wordy caskets! Our sun shall preen down its wacky-woo, shimmy-shoo, and as the feast melts, an educated guess shall never fail to leap and snort at the stink of death.

JANUARY 28, 1997

They say if you can't beat 'em, join 'em. They never say what to do when you can't beat 'em *or* join 'em. This seems quite an oversight, given the predominance of the scenario. They also don't say what to do if you can both beat 'em *and* join 'em. Would beating 'em preclude joining 'em, or vice-versa? In my case, I feel that I can beat 'em but can't join 'em. Should I feel satisfied with this?

JANUARY 29, 1997

Could it be that everything that *is* is just a funny after-taste? That brings us to the terrible question of what is funny. Certainly the body hanging down or bobbing is funny, and perhaps too any sounds associated with the noticing of it. But those sounds—that's a different kind of funny. And those sounds get stuck on themselves eventually. Then a meal with no funny after-taste seems absolutely necessary.

JANUARY 30, 1997

If I were royalty I would want a Biggie and a hundred plain burgers. I would throw away the buns and lay the burgers side by side on the sidewalk so as to form a bed. I would take off all my clothes and lie down in the bed with my Biggie. As people passed by, I would say, "Behold the meaty bed of royalty! Behold the final Biggie!" And I would relax there until I was arrested.

JANUARY 31, 1997

The urge to belong. I'm so jealous when the employees speak to one another in that *knowing* way. I always look away as if I didn't care, as if their easy affection with one another was the last thing on my mind. But why do I yearn so persistently to be included—what would *being included* mean? An implicit motherland? A small drink of blood for my hungry shade?

FEBRUARY 1, 1997

I fear we will be captured soon. I think really it will come
as a relief. To finally be able to talk about what we've done!
I think it's gone on too long. I certainly won't miss having
to act all lady-like all day long. I won't miss the Glacier-
Song either. Just think, when we're captured, it won't be
our problem anymore! Or do you think we will hurt forever,
not knowing that real, negligible progress?

February 2, 1997

I'm pleasantly disappointed. This gives me the opportunity to mingle. Whenever I get a form that asks for my occupation I check *Other* and write in: *I'm mingling*. People think of mingling as easy, but it's really very difficult. It only becomes easy when one stops trying to mingle and starts something else—say, seduction. But my intention is steadfast and pure. I intend to mingle.

FEBRUARY 3, 1997

I tried to order a Biggie coffee today. It couldn't be done. I felt sort of childish asking, like my request betrayed my ignorance in the matter. Ironically, nothing could be further from the truth; *I know*—believe me I do—how wrong it is to have a coffee of that size (I know too that I would have never gone through with it). It's sort of scary, but the truth is: I really don't know why I asked.

FEBRUARY 4, 1997

The animals don't coincide. What a mess! If only it was that simple. The worst part is that it's loud. And it may not be that the mess is loud—it may be that *each animal* is loud, and that the mess, the uncoincidental arena, is only ever as quiet as it is hungry. The theory all along on our part has been that it just needs a good cleaning and it will quiet down. That it's a nice place, the animals notwithstanding.

FEBRUARY 5, 1997

I never see deliveries being made. I'm glad. I harbor no creationism naiveté, as though fries or burgers were simply *born* as what they are. No, it's just that I already understand that these things are conjured and what matters now is not *how* but *for what*? The conjuring isn't *interesting* to me except insofar as it reveals its ultimate utility, the one it cannot possibly succeed in.

FEBRUARY 6, 1997

In my mind, Wendy, you are like someone in a silent movie.
Too slow when you're still, but then too fast when you move.
And you have that same blank introspection, as if struggling
to convey something—perhaps the reason for your ridiculous
outfit. I wish I could help you tell me. It's not your fault—
it's the fault of this movie, my mind. It's a silent movie and
will never be otherwise.

FEBRUARY 7, 1997

Wendy, soon I will kiss you passionately in the cunt and hold on tight to nothing. I will tongue your eyelids and your belly like they were one and the same. I will lay my dick across your belly and ask you where your mouth is. I will find your mouth. I will escort us both into a place of disintegrating requirements. And no one will come and save us.

FEBRUARY 8, 1997

Wendy, will you not even poke me? Not even a slow poke? I wonder why you treat me so. Am I a wooden board? Am I to be thought of as a simple wooden board? Come on, just give me a slow poke. I'm not a wooden board, honey. Come on, just poke me like you used to. Just a slow poke. Look into my eyes—are these the eyes of a wooden board?

FEBRUARY 9, 1997

Like a filthy hound in a time of elegant drawbridges, I ache with hope. Like a remembered fuck, I coat the story-teller with day-darkness. Like a tourist's camera accidentally dropped overboard, I tumble into darkness without capturing it. Like a famous gun, I continually assert an incongruous sense of the ordinary. Like an inarticulate indictment, I outlast every ecstasy.

FEBRUARY 10, 1997

One watches the others order. An aesthetics develops. It's
not the worst thing that could happen. Yes, a weariness
lurks, often, in the obvious next step—the dream of a school.
The only thing worse than endeavoring to create a school
is endeavoring to maintain a school. Which is why I like,
above all, those customers who, in the middle of their order
and quite without warning, change their minds.

FEBRUARY 11, 1997

My desire causes an order and then I wait as it gets carried over into the real. This carrying over produces a delicious fact, which the order cannot have signified. The order drifts away, then, from the delicious fact—drifts into *mere* words. The delicious fact, in turn, causes its own pulverization. Factless, the dreadful noise of preparation continues for a whole other order.

FEBRUARY 12, 1997

If I had the money I would buy a slave, but only if I had
enough to buy a master as well. Not a master for my slave,
but a master for myself. *I* would be my slave's master. I
would call my slave "Bucket," and I would ask my master
to call me "Bucket," too. The countryside would ring with
calls of "Bucket!" and with the irresolute gentility of
simultaneous whippings.

FEBRUARY 13, 1997

Taint nuffin long the woods no mo. Taint a breevin stitch.
Whut choo wants, Mr. Woods-man? Want some Breevin-
Stitch-Pie? How you gonna make it? You goin hongry,
Woods. You an me bofe uv us. Taint nuffin long the woods
no more. Taint a bref of a bug even.

FEBRUARY 14, 1997

It has taken me this long to confess that I am not a fan of the salad bar. That is, to *openly* confess it. Surely my silence on the matter has created an impression already. I suppose I've been ashamed to speak. I have this sense that in speaking I will be led to something embarrassing, something at odds with the uniquely liberal persona I prance about in. This, though, this letter, is a good first step.

FEBRUARY 15, 1997

Today there was a dog in the road. He just stood there looking at oncoming cars. I thought he might bark, but no. He just looked. I could imagine the irritated drivers saying, "what is he *doing*?" He was just looking. I felt such a comradery. Myself and this dog, standing our ground in the midst of a brutal foreign routine, unimpressed with it, unwilling to cower before its fast disappearing machines.

FEBRUARY 17, 1997

Building Slippage, I sing of Nothing. Shall we build an Again, or shall we hate the Already from which its singer must begin? Everyone says, *just sing!* as though singing would, this time, not begin to construct an Again. But maybe hatred of the Already could be *love* of Nothing. Maybe the white-hot bowels of Forgetting are always already in love with an Again that cannot be organized.

FEBRUARY 18, 1997

I believe I'm actually going to have to be strapped down.
One comes to a point where one has NOT come to a
point—where one will soon have to MAKE a point to be
anywhere at all. You had better send someone to strap me
down. And if you wouldn't mind, I'd like to have some tests
done. I don't care what you attempt to determine, just that
you do it politely and that you never give up hope.

February 19, 1997

Nodding, bleeding out as steadily as anyone ever, the go-getters uphold their migration. Sometimes it's even beautiful—their freedom from thought and their vigilant impulse to nestle further in to the flock. Lord, let them nestle well—do not leave one behind! Let them pass, squawking, drifting blankly in their beautiful rows—let them find that warm nest far away and breed and die. And let their brood return to us as welcome criminals.

FEBRUARY 21, 1997

Motherfuck everything but the weather. Let the weather come through and and through and through. Your pores are not yours. Motherfuck everything but the weather and the ones who let the weather come through and through and through. The ones whose pores are not deeded or stored. Those are your brothers and sisters.

FEBRUARY 23, 1997

The enormity of a Biggie: is it something we can really understand? Our desire for a Biggie isn't at all practical. If anything, we desire a Biggie because it isn't practical—*because it is too big*. To understand this—to understand all at once that it's too big to fit inside oneself—is to restore oneself to Sense, which, in its endless failure to consume the fullness of what is real, learns to at least respect it.

February 25, 1997

Standing there waiting for fries, me and this older man. He said to me, "You'd think they had to grow the potatoes!" I replied, a bit too loud, "Daddy fucked me!" The man seemed angry—I don't think he understood what I meant. It's as though we were on the same field, playing different games. He, however, seemed not able to understand that a different game from his own was possible.

FEBRUARY 26, 1997

so troubling is the lull in this carriage that the authorities have outnumbered themselves and required that the seasons repeat their intentions until they are less meaningless than the colors for which they rush—so spectacular is the comfort of the seat that the authorities are able to overlook the seasons' failure to meet requirements and to feel the meaningless rush as an impromptu massage

FEBRUARY 27, 1997

First, I became very ill. Then I blessed Your holy Name.
Then I sang Your glory. Then I received the guarantee, the
bonus. I climbed out of the pit of darkness into the rapture
of simple obedience, and I was saved. Then I realized it
didn't matter what I said or did. I was relieved. Then I
smashed Your image and Your word and returned to a life
of abundant health and leisure.

FEBRUARY 28, 1997

The aged have a long continent moment, cherishing the salt of a fry and the familiarity of a spouse's voice. Children thrust through a good pulverizing. Their mothers recede. Businessmen titter in a frugal pause. Their mothers recede. The unemployed mow the massive lawn that is their mind. The newly deaf hear the mowers all day long. The paraplegics smile.

MARCH 1, 1997

Nuscle up to some Downhome Stanky. Must Fields proposing names for the Rut that feeds em' and eats em' up. Shut up already! Ain't we got minds of our owns? Is it for us or for the Must Fields to nuscle up to the Stanky Rut? Ain't we got nuscles of our owns? The Must Fields need be silenced altogether and with complacency. Ain't no other way to get back Downhome.

MARCH 2, 1997

Barely able to move today, some sort of virus. Almost decided not to come in. Could only stomach a Coke. Still, glad I came. Glad I limped sweating into the loud line. I have come to appreciate, from afar, the force that stands volume, bright. The booth as good as a bed, at first—until I think of a bed. Satisfaction, for the sick, comes so fast and hard it doesn't register.

MARCH 3, 1997

It's as if I'm being suffocated by large blocks of ice. The bottoms of my feet, my back, my face, my thighs—I press at the ice. Each effort succeeds in postponing suffocation by establishing a pain that suffocation cannot contain. The pain hems and haws in the suffocation, and joyful is the silence of its disappearing crest. I wish I had been born without limbs.

MARCH 5, 1997

As I get older, it gets harder to keep myself from touching the other customers in line. When I'm feverish, as I am today, this is especially true. You obese, you aged smokers (lucky ones!), you tall lonely kids, sluggish clean women, you men standing guard all day and all night over your own flavorful stupor, how beautiful you are to the touch in my mind!

MARCH 6, 1997

My life is not a story. I'd like to apologize for that. I know
what a nuisance it is for you. *I've tried* to make my life into a
story—you know I have—but every time I've been returned
to the heart of the city in chains. I accept this as the fated
role I am to play. I wait here, in chains, for you to pass by.
For you to look out of the story and into me, into the way
I'm bound, unsheltered, guilty of nothing.

MARCH 7, 1997

I was lured out slowly, by a series of toys. Each new toy appeared to be a new step toward establishing me in an eternal state of play. The *insufficiency* of each discarded toy was always hidden by this coming play. A pile developed, though, and couldn't, in time, be hidden. After awhile I stopped getting new toys. I was interested only in the pile, the insufficiency. I sit with it even now; *I'm learning not to play*.

MARCH 8, 1997

Savages knew better this ground we merely count on. They gathered it with ornate stabbing shouts—without success, but then success was not yet a possible delusion. They were just glad to wake up in the chance to stab. How wrong we are to be sad—how cowardly our faith in the real estate business! We have forgotten: *God always gives us a burden that we can't handle.*

MARCH 9, 1997

The tenuous throb delights in exposing itself. I am its forever unsuspecting dupe. Which is to say, I have to this day always feigned surprise. It's getting harder, though. I'm in no danger of being found out—no, the tenuous throb is too vain to dream of itself as unsurprising. It's more that I have come to be fascinated with the unthinkability of the alternative: *if not surprise, then what?*

MARCH 10, 1997

I like a full, hard bowel movement when I shit at Wendy's.
I don't really worry about privacy anymore—in fact, I sort
of like the company of strangers. They make the decisive
moment—at once the gripping and the release—more
resonant. I like that someone is there to hear me whisper,
O yeah baby give it to me. The ambiguity of this exchange
is refreshing in so many ways.

MARCH 13, 1997

No further goes the drain—SUCH NOISE! At the time of my disappearance, the circus was painful. (The drain is not absolute after all.) This pain that resists the drain—is it the circus? No, the circus is less intentional, less romantic, than that—it just moves. The pain calls after it wherever it goes. At the time of my disappearance, SUCH NOISE! The circus drains, painless.

MARCH 14, 1997

As I look around the restaurant at all the beautiful folks enjoying themselves, I wonder what catastrophe awaits each one. Young man, will your heart explode? Will your intestines fill with blood? Perhaps a seizure on a boat in the middle of a lake. The sun shining down. The stars concealed once and for all. I always feel less anxious when I recognize that the collision is already well under way.

MARCH 16, 1997

Wendy is beautiful within, not beyond, description. So it goes with the dead, the natives of the thriving sign. Beauty's nothing more than weather damage—the sign's fading, crumbling, blinking out. Beauty is de-scription, not in-scription. Beauty, as such, is endless, so long as knowledge of the tremendous impotence of inscription does not stop the dead from rising to meet its hideous precondition.

MARCH 18, 1997

I maybe ain't so good at speechifying, but I can sure as fuck split my head open and deliver its real hardworking matter to the hungry air! I can also turn furniture upside down (if it isn't too heavy). The fucking point is clear: I may not be an individual, but I'm still a force to be reckoned with. Forget this, and my bloody head will be all over your fucking upside down furniture.

MARCH 19, 1997

The land of the tongue is no land at all. Each thing jumps out of its comatose mother and refuses to decide where it will sleep. Nothing is always under way and never any closer to completion. Wendy's is not just a stop along the way to Nothing. Wendy's is a way of blocking that way and restoring the tongue to its definitive project: knowing, at its own expense, the false eternity of the womb.

MARCH 20, 1997

If you need someone to hold the fort down, you need someone dead. I'm your man. If I'm not dead, no one is. There's no fort I cannot hold down. It's impossible to convey just how dead I am and how secure the fort would be in my care. Perhaps seeing it evaporate in the care of someone far less dead than myself would make you understand. But then, there is no understanding without the fort.

MARCH 21, 1997

Dumbfounded before the slaughter, and so, special. Shall we consider the dumbfounding? No, the dumbfounding is over. We shall consider a memory of the dumbfounding. We shall tease a memory out from the slaughter-bed, and from the sleeping slaughterers' songs. We have a lot of work to do. Insofar as we succeed in it, we establish one thing: being not special.

MARCH 22, 1997

Today I ordered a hot wet pussy-dickhead shake with eyes
and tongues. "We're all out," says the brave young employee.
"You must've just run out," says I, "because I can still smell
it." "Yep, just sold the last one," says the brave young
employee. "Why don't you make more?" asks I. At this
point the manager came over. "Is there a problem?" says
he. "You're out of hot wet pussy-dickhead shakes," says I.

MARCH 23, 1997

A good long blood-bath in the works. Clean off the counter and the tables and the bathroom walls and get ready. Stop *blaming* one another. Stop worrying over "fair" division of labor. The flock is too sick, at every point, to take such worries seriously. Listen to your "private" parts hanging down and/or gaping! Our being *in the offing* indicates, above all, that we are *still on*.

MARCH 24, 1997

I press my forehead to the cool table-top. A feeling of well-being like a wedge driven into the glare of the devoured meal. Everything's hidden in plain view. My heart, my face, my bowels—all enlisted in the tedious delight of the wedge. This delight brings me to where it's too late. All that's left for me is well-being and death. It's never too late for well-being and death.

MARCH 25, 1997

The dining grave bores its faces until they can't stand it—
until they think fast— and something important is
fabricated, undersung, and quickly abolished. Null
successors squirming in the quickness try not to hear the
undersinging that predicts them, try to pass laws against
abolition, against fast thinking, against boredom, against
graves—in short, against all importance.

MARCH 26, 1997

Shall I put my penis on the counter? But what would it really accomplish? Would it change the world? Would it change me, or the attendant employees? No, no, and no. But should we judge an activity by whether or not it *changes* something? That would imply evolution as pre-determined and full of specific purpose. My penis on the counter is resistance; it demonstrates evolution's indeterminate willfulness.

MARCH 27, 1997

We shall swing by the Anal Ranch, pick up the Lord, and we shall have a Butt-Fuck Week-End. The Lord will have a Biggie. Our faces will be dripping with hot cum and we shall notice the way muscle is. The Lord will be our Butt-Fuck Buddy and we will be the Butt-Fuck Buddies of the Lord. But never shall it spill, the Biggie of the Lord—not ever.

MARCH 30, 1997

Sometimes I think it's all a jar of scabs. Then I taste the meaty goodness of a mustard-only burger and I think *it can't be*—I think: *this is too good to be a jar of scabs. Where there's a jar, there's always an owner, and there's no owner here. It's more miraculous heap than jar. And it may be scabs, but not only scabs.* To say *it's only scabs* is to romanticize the heap.

MARCH 31, 1997

To this sunny day I surrender all my good intentions. I will have my meal and then go on without them. That means I will breathe, or something will breathe through me. I'll notice bright patches waning. I'll notice my meal in my gut, the world's shadows swimming in the swimming surface of my eye. Surely this sunny day will care for the world's shadows, and for all of the quiet parasites therein.

April 1, 1997 (April Fools Day)

Such a hot day, my balls hanging *so far* down, I can't help
but think of the chosen one, the one whose face was made
to bear witness to this hanging down—the lips, the soft
cheeks, the softly closed eyes, the eyelashes, the chin, the
face fated to absorb that delicate pressure—my balls being
dragged slowly, slowly, across the forehead, down the brim
of the nose…. *Where art thou? Where art thou not?*

APRIL 4, 1997

One is accused of *sensationalism* when one focuses on pain. Rightly so when one is using pain to re-create a pre-existing sensation. But in truth pain has never been before, exactly, and its shadow has always concealed its coming fullness. To know this is to haul out the most fundamental question a speaking animal can attempt. The question is not: *what is creating pain?* The question is: *what is pain creating?*

APRIL 5, 1997

Often I come to Wendy's looking like who'd a' thought it.
This is only ever an indication that I am still appropriate,
which is to say, still overdetermined by a fascination with
the meaty crux. You can call me a scientist if you want to,
but if you do, you don't understand how hungry I am.
Sometimes I am so hungry I wear a white belt with white
pants.

APRIL 7, 1997

This fear of dying—does it make sense? I look forward to news of the final descent, wherein I will gain unlimited access to drugs and to being cared for. Since we have come to understand how thoroughly artificial our significance is, and since we have at the same time invented great new drugs to ease pain, I see no other conclusion: this is the most wonderful time ever to be dying!

APRIL 8, 1997

Sometimes I think of Wendy's as a library without books.
Without records, magazines, maps, or videos. Without a
rare books room, and without an Information desk. As such,
it is the most pleasant library I've ever visited. It offers one
text—on reserve and on view. This text explicitly organizes
the way we feed ourselves. And it allows us to act as though
a greater significance has never been attempted.

APRIL 9, 1997

Let's lay all our drills out in the open. How else shall we ever come to know the full smothering brilliance of the gloss? This is no time to tolerate useless testimony! This is no time to explore the mammy system as if it could be regulated more effectively! This is a time for looking the other way! This is a time for leaving infants on stoops! This is a time, above all, for relaxation.

APRIL 10, 1997

Resolute dissonance. I love the way the grass punches
through the dream of a fixed ground and burns itself alive.
The punch has a sound, as does the dream and the burning
alive. They keep one another. They are a war. It's not a war
that can be won. They conflict—they inflict one another. I
love the way the grass punches through the dream of a fixed
ground and burns itself alive.

APRIL 12, 1997

Methinks a walking trunk comes back to haunt its mother
The Music. Comes back without limbs in the night and
will not sing along. This is how we get a mother on the run,
a music afraid of the predictability of its own solitary regress.
The trunk, although it will never sing, is thrilled by its
distant regressive mother's fear, and is moved to dance in it.
In the night, without limbs.

APRIL 13, 1997

It's good Wendy's offers no clock. No ticking stick on a stone. The day writhes, at Wendy's, without anxious narrative—without the tiresome business of documenting the insignificant variation in its tiny silences. Time is restored to the day's writhing—restored, that is, to an active drawing of it. One draws upon a drawing of a drawing until one senses what one cannot draw.

APRIL 14, 1997

The line today was too long and the register girl seemed bitter the whole time. Her obvious bitterness made my waiting in line feel spiteful. The spite was twofold—there was the initial spite, which was only a seeming, and then there was the spite I felt as a reaction to being implicated in this seeming. That is, the false emotion, in recognizing itself as false, seemed to create the possibility of its being true.

APRIL 15, 1997

If I was in the audience of a talk show and I was lucky enough to be chosen to make a comment, I would say: "You can't have your cake and eat it too." The rest of the audience would applaud and the people on stage would have to face up to the harsh reality of their situation. Given a second chance to comment, I would say, "The Lord rapes us in mysterious ways."

APRIL 17, 1997

At Wendy's when someone's pissing next to me I look over at his penis and then look down at mine and it always seems that, although a meaningful discussion between myself and this other is clearly out of the question, our penises would very much enjoy and greatly benefit from a discussion. And I'm always saddened by the strange surety of their silences.

APRIL 18, 1997

Nowadays a corporation need support a *cause* now and then to demonstrate its investment in "the future." Wendy's could launch a "Catheters For The Birds" campaign. The goal would be to capture, catheterize, and rehabilitate into nature all birds. This is a perfect project; even as it yearns for a better world, it at the same time shows how yearning itself almost imperceptibly binds us into countless discomforts.

APRIL 19, 1997

It is rare for a baby to be so bad that it is sentenced to be hanged, and even rarer for the sentence to be carried out, and yet, when a baby is hung, what a pleasant surprise it is for the passersby. Even the passerby whose arms and legs are bound is able to inch up close enough to the tiny, swaying, villainous nugget of softness and know, with his bare cheek, the threshold through which real evil sinks away.

APRIL 20, 1997

I stand above each activity and judge its rate of completion.
Waiting in line, eating. There are two judgments: *too slow*
and *too fast*. There is no *just right*—or rather, when an
activity's rate of completion is *just right* it is impossible for
me to stand above that activity. I am compelled to stand *in*
it, *as* it. I must conclude, then, that insofar as I am a judge,
I am a hanging judge.

APRIL 21, 1997

A chaste glaring pretends to us. Fuck you, I say. Fuck you.

APRIL 22, 1997

I know that when I'm dead they'll put my picture up on the wall. This solaces me. Beside my name it will say: *I ate here, as here ate me.* In life one moves with difficulty through the dim muscular masses of by-standers in an effort to glimpse the passing parade; in death one is thrust into that parade — one is fixed in it and moves with it through the dim muscular masses like a picture on a wall.

APRIL 23, 1997

The trouble is that the spilling out learns to gather itself even as it continues to spill! There's no *cure* for the spilling; greeting cards may deny this, but such denial is never, as it claims, a definitive gathering. Rather, it's an indication of how *tired* the gatherer has become—and how *aware* of gathering's futility. On my greeting cards, therefore, I always write, "Hoping for a cure ruins what little we have."

APRIL 24, 1997

Evening arises and I feel myself in the threshold of my face.
My face is a threshold—I look out through it. Inside is dark,
paled by the panting shock of mimesis. Outside is just
another inside, but less pale and more conducive to bouts
of brutal dancing. From my face, I stand and watch. The
dancing intrigues me, but so does the pale dark. I don't
know in which way my destiny lies.

APRIL 25, 1997

Some would say that these letters are bringing about no *real* change. While it's true that no change will be directly apparent, how silly to conclude that they will lead to no change at all! This is to reduce the incredibly complex pressures and residues of history to a simple series of discrete events. If history is the recollection of a martyr's face, it requires time—it requires the fidgeting testimony of the whole attendant mob.

APRIL 26, 1997

Wendy's sits next to the fullest possible manifestation of our casual rushing vacancy. This is well and good; I like to think of this vacancy, this busy thoroughfare, as my mother. It has certainly birthed me. Wendy's is that space wherein I have attempted to leave my mother, and to come to some kind of independent fullness. That fullness looms like a room full of obsolete tools.

APRIL 27, 1997

If we are to collect the gathering and to sort it in the naked
probing fashion, we must be willing to see the resulting
heap as the bitch of a completely exhausted naked prober.
The naked prober, because he is completely exhausted, will
not deny that this is true, and we may mistakenly understand
his silence as resplendent. But real resplendence is never
silent and has no bitch.

APRIL 28, 1997

Sold into rest. Humped about the head by giggling eunuchs. If only I could move — if only I could drag myself from this tiny cot and find an open grave to crawl into. In an open grave I would not be humped about the head by all these gigglers and I could perform what rest I still owe.

APRIL 29, 1997

When I get good pills I often neglect to shower. Neglect is always necessary, one way or another. And anyway, I like the way my head gets after a few days of not showering— it's like I have a much keener sense of my skull—how truly perceptive its various surfaces are. To feel *that* perceptive is to feel *glorious, glamorous*—fully innocent within a fully sensible execution.

APRIL 30, 1997

As I eat I like to look into the sun glaring on the big
windows. I look until there is a large black spot in my eye.
I believe this spot is God. God never speaks—It's just there,
a dead spot in the mechanism that reminds me it *is* a
mechanism. I sleep there, in God, until It fades away, until
the mechanism heals and again there is no God. Then I go
back and look into the glare.

MAY 2, 1997

Non-stop beauty now, among the baby-snatchers. I am forever starting over. Is this, perhaps, for you? Do I know you? Didn't you emancipate the colonies? Jesus! You have so many babies! Good lord! Would someone please demythologize me!

MAY 3, 1997

I detest the mode. All the intrepid, able-bodied heroes in the history of human enthusiasm leave me no choice. In the end I will have to go and hide. I will hide out in the open, where no one thinks to look. I will have all my limbs with me. I will hide behind my limbs if I feel like someone is looking. I will sing louder, as if no one is really here.

MAY 4, 1997

Tell us about your visit—WE CARE! Often I have been hesitant to send you my thoughts; without this *unconditional* interest of yours, would I have had the courage to bring some of my visits to language? You don't say, *tell us about your pleasant visit*—no, you CARE, and caring means tending to the real visit in all its difficulty. Knowing before-hand that you "appreciate my comments" means so much to me—thank you.

MAY 5, 1997

The bleeders in the horizon somehow procreate, somehow keep up their vegetarian moan. The horizon doesn't bleed — don't let anyone tell you the horizon bleeds. And don't let them tell you we need to "understand" how the bleeders procreate either. Such "understanding" only ever leads to the ridiculous attempt to establish an "honest" chaperone.

May 6, 1997

Negligent eye-keeper, you underestimate me. However much you underfeed me, however many whole days you leave me alone in the cage, however small you make my chance, whatever force you exert toward my suffocation — you underestimate me. My blindness is equal to yours.

MAY 7, 1997

Thought, truly beheld, is just anal erotica. Thought is a giant dildo in the dark, working its way into the ass of its beloved, its complex pet. The pet cries out in delight and/or anxiety. The cry varies until it is speech, until it is light thrown on to penetration. Speech brings thought—a giant dildo in our mind-ass-hole—to light. It lets the dildo know we're still interested, or at least awake.

May 8, 1997

There is no *through*—this isn't a maze! There's no curtain, no *other side*. The *other side* is just a bed-time story for frigid necrophiliacs. It lets them fall back to sleep. It lets them dissociate themselves from endless horny waking. Their fears of waking, however, may be well founded. I mean, necrophilia leads inevitably to other more dangerous practices. Love of the living body, for instance.

MAY 10, 1997

I guess the earth is crusted with what—blood, piss, shit,
bone? I like to think of it as eyes and scales piled deep,
piled smart enough to bask. Then I feel like I'm headed in
the right direction—one always wants to head *toward* the
basking. What would it mean for someone to head
intentionally *away from* the basking? To answer this
question is to have already moved away from the basking.

MAY 11, 1997

Bulging foray—interrupted!!! If it please the court, stop looking at me. The aborted database exceeds even the least plausible of my faces and the sounds my faces can make. Therein lies the plunder. The plunder isn't plausible! Dear lord, we're in this for good. We're the fucking *ing*!!! *Ing ing ing ing ing ing ing* with just the white spaces (the nouns) drowned and drowning inbetween.

MAY 12, 1997

I like to think that, deep down, we're all surgeons. And not just any surgeons, but surgeons on a doomed airship. That is, there are grounds for postponing surgery, and we all know it. We know it, but we don't want to accept it. To accept it would mean giving ourselves over to drowning in the impasse at the heart of every honest consultation.

MAY 13, 1997

I refuse to entertain, as I have said, the simplistic notion of *the visit itself*. To entertain such an idea is to assume a historical scene wherein images are definite and definitely affixed to *real* substances. Such a definite affixing is the habit of lazy brutal folks — not me. For me, a visit occurs when imagery coheres with reality in such a way as to make definition start all over.

May 14, 1997

So many minor procedures at once—I don't know how your employees maintain their delightful sheen. It's as though there is something in them that yearns for this challenge, juggling more, juggling faster, until there is no one there, until the juggling itself is the only thing, a vacant momentum. It's sad to think it has such a small audience as myself.

MAY 15, 1997

We inject the items. The items are only temporarily subject to us as we inject them. We may in some sense be subject to the items, but only insofar as they exist within injection. The items are never objects and they are never going to be. We are certainly thrown, but not *toward* or *under* the items. We're thrown *through* the items and inject them, imperfectly, in an effort to slow our passing out of them.

MAY 16, 1997

This is to respectfully ask that you watch me pee. I have the feeling that I am peeing wrong, and as it stands, what's to stop me? I suspect that there must be many others in this predicament. Once one realizes how absolutely alone one is when one is alone in a "restroom," one is inevitably tempted to pee in a wrong way. To create this temptation seems to me an act of remarkable malice.

MAY 17, 1997

Allowing it to shine, I provide dark beds for the dying sound of waking. I will not work for the sleeping faces out to prolong its life. I will not even agree that it has a life. My intention is to make it comfortable, the dying sound of waking. This may mean telling it stories that aren't true. It may mean entertaining it with my own death. Clearly, if it is to shine, sacrifices must be made.

MAY 18, 1997

Never anyone willing to talk about it or maybe not even possible, that. A sense that one tags along hemorrhaging after the "not physical and not mental." The simple motion which has always already and is already gone. Maybe impossible but what solace is impossibility? I guess the hemorrhaging is something.

MAY 19, 1997

The thriving banks of fluorescence. No withdrawals here—
only the useless growth of interest. I feel good about the
establishment of complete light. It allows me to course fully
dangling into the given accident. So much argument over
what's truly *given*, the dangling or the accident that severs it.
What really matters is the coursing, which is not given, but
taken.

MAY 20, 1997

I'd like to have my muscles removed. Resume the inanimate.
Wendy's allows me to extract myself from the retarded
narcissism of animal thrivings. I sit still in a warm booth
and get thought. All movement wants, in the end, is stillness;
the animate is just the failure of movement to get what it
wants—one sleeping body. The road to heaven is paved
with meat: the road to meat is not paved at all.

MAY 21, 1997

I can remember when I had no hair on my legs. I can remember lying in the bathtub in a sort of trance, deeply aware of the fact that my legs would *grow*—would not remain what they so clearly were in that moment. Looking at my legs now, I wonder how I ever pulled myself out of that trance. I guess one can get used to absolutely anything.

MAY 22, 1997

Slathered over against tranq-bath songs. Never under, never sown. Or, concurrently, slatted back with ruined-tush-image, for which the tranq-bath songs try to die. Songs cannot die, though, exactly, and anyone actually slathered over against them would have to agree, or at least confess that the question is not interesting. What is interesting is the under, the sown, the tush itself, which never appears.

MAY 23, 1997

Parts of cities, brain, smeared into the gums. Let's reminisce.
Daddy with his tingling chute. Mommy fidgeting toward
compliance. The talk of speaking of names that surrounded
them, then. And then, and then, and then. Those who
hesitate are found.

May 25, 1997

Wendy's needs a stench area. People like a stench. Their initial reaction—pained withdrawal—is always quickly followed by cautious fascination. A stench is a *stink* that has found a way to *entrench* itself. It is metaphor: abstraction *digs in* to a real body and decomposes it to the point of presence. People like a stench because it mimics their own truest moments.

MAY 26, 1997

Penises still sprouting in all the familiar places. Where do we go from here? Do we allow the sperm banks to employ us in their deepening beauracracy or do we commit ourselves to simply coming upon where we are? If we are the former, we are that which resists the sterile raping flow. If we are the latter, we are its priests, or its pin-up girls, or both.

MAY 27, 1997

I gentle each time sunlight comes. I don't mean that I'm any less brutal in how I mount it. I mean I've become more of a spectator at the mounting. The more you become a spectator, the more you gentle. It isn't necessarily a bad thing, this gentling. So long as your mounting continues to mount. So long, that is, as you resist what is inevitable, what is *natural*, the sunlight mounting you.

MAY 28, 1997

At any given "point," one can look "back" and say, *what was that?* But then one can never answer sufficiently. One can say, "I had a burger, there was the woman with the hump, cold sweat made me itch," and still one hasn't summed up why one existed or where. This *why* and this *where* in fact become obscured by every seeking of them. In speaking, we only ever lose where we are—we do not secure it.

May 29, 1997

Who in truth does not *love* the pitter-patter of The Sick on their picturesque way to an automatic Mommy? At Wendy's I prick up my ears and that way comes back to me. It's so foreign, so breathtakingly inconsequential. And it seems everyone is going that way. Why can't I go that way? Is it because I need to find the way picturesque, and can only do so from afar?

MAY 30, 1997

Demerol today, and lots of coffee. I feel good. The way a
log in a fire sometimes looks like it must feel good—like
it's gotten once and for all past its resistance to the force
that means to make it submit to its own physical fact. Like
it's learned how to enjoy the clean deep hate for which all
tending struggles. Like it's learned that there is a best way to
go out.

JUNE 1, 1997

At Wendy's I often feel like an ex-prisoner-of-war, decades after my release, returning to the prison in which I was detained. The country is nothing like it was back then. The prison has been made into a tourist spot. I feel a kind of maddening sadness—not at my imprisonment, or at some lack of justice, but because I see how easily, how endlessly, an evil country escapes us.

JUNE 2, 1997

If we were to excavate the "teeth" in my intestines, what would we *do* with them? And more importantly, how could we ever explain to them why they were being removed? How could we explain it to ourselves! Sure, it would be a great pleasure, at first, to bring them into the light, and to show them off, but would we not tire of them as quickly as we tire of every other thing that does not work?

JUNE 3, 1997

I took my Frosty into the bathroom and sat it on the floor. I pulled my pants down, got down on all fours, and buried the tip of my cock in the cold brown swirl. Then I forced my cock and balls all the way into the cup, Frosty spilling on to the floor. Then I thought sexy thoughts. My erection slowly forced more Frosty on to the floor. This is the real test of a drink's thickness.

JUNE 4, 1997

How pained the thorough clean becomes in the dream-shinnying of any warm afternoon's light. We are thrust into a lazy retreat but forget, almost immediately, which way the retreat is moving. We may now be moving directly toward the enemy. And so, our joy is always only how lazy we can get, and how unclean.

June 8, 1997

the present hidden by a hurting heap—only laceration pleases it, prepares it for neglect—I'm the nothing-blade in the hurting heap—I drag sleep by the hair until it speaks—I don't hear what it says—I'm the hurting heap with the nothing-blade sleeping me apart—I am prepared for neglect—I am prepared for nothing but neglect

JUNE 10, 1997

It's fair to say the way to day is a balmy reservoir. At least for us, and for the other more complicated tubes. The noise seems less. I don't know if this is an indication of efficiency or malfunction. Oh but then malfunction always lets slip that efficiency was just the dream bravery of a slave without a master. Man, there's no plan, let alone plantation.

JUNE 11, 1997

Whosoever sucks my dick sucks the dicks of the least of my brothers. Or at least that is my hope. Cold and numb upon a blazing raft, I approach paralysis with the highest hope. There are large splinters of moment, after all, yet unpulverized. Between hot and cold there is a simple deaf slope. That's the place for sucking dicks, for hope, and for the joyful end of re-cognition.

JUNE 12, 1997

HELP! (this helmet is fusing with my skull)

JUNE 13, 1997

Let's say Wendy's is an airplane. Traveling at ten thousand feet. Let's say there's no landing gear and nowhere to land. And fuel is limited. And one has a general idea of when the fuel is going to run out. Given this knowledge, is *travel* really the right word? And if not travel, then what? One sees one's life quite differently when one knows it isn't going to land.

JUNE 15, 1997

I plummet, I actually plummet. I had feared it, the prospect
of it, plummeting. But with drugs it isn't bad. It's almost
nice to plummet and to know one is plummeting, and at
the same time to have a good feeling deep down. I guess
someone could accuse me of playing the martyr. That's not
accurate, though. If there's a martyr in this, he's the show
and I'm the audience.

JUNE 17, 1997

A tall woman—at least 6'6"—ordered a large Coke with no ice. When people do this, I assume they've brought ice, and that they'll proceed to pour their soda into it. But this woman had brought no ice. She sat in a booth and drank her Coke just like that—not a speck of ice. I was appalled. This Freak Show is too long.

JUNE 19, 1997

Pain and sleep and dull flocks of noise stitching them together with what flesh there is. Notice how deep the flocks carry the needle into one and then the other. One gets the impression it will fall all apart in time. And though quite impossible to believe, this impression is nevertheless the whole truth.

JUNE 20, 1997

So life is a dream from which we never wake. Perhaps we gain a sense of the bodies that endlessly precede it, but we cannot leap "in" to them because that sense is so brief (it's a kind of seizure) and in it we are given to understand that we don't have the bodies—the bodies have us. We are also given to understand that the bodies never really intended to have us, and don't intend to keep us.

JUNE 21, 1997

Happy humpy problem-grave, do your incomes rhyme? I know the work you do—do you know mine? Happy humping dying-day, have you burst your eye? I reduce the knowing store—I damage what you buy. Happy humpy shattered-glare, must you keep a spy? I wish I could speak with you—I wish I could make you cry.

JUNE 22, 1997

The urinals are the only point of contact—albeit buried—
with the unsewn. Must the moistness matter so indirectly?
We all say, "if I was in a position of power…" *but there is no
position of power!!* The moistness shall behave as it likes,
and we shall do nothing. We shall continue to sew, as if our
sewing was going to soon become some sort of revolutionary
deterrent—as if soon a great smock would grow on our
hearts!

JUNE 23, 1997

Mumb-drool erections smothering Attention at the behest of a towering devouring one-time-only Sleeping Face. Smothering predictably—they are indeed drool—but at the same time with a quickness, an ability to found themselves, already erect, in the fictive interior, causing the invaluable embarrassment of its sudden debut. (There is a fry on the floor.)

June 28, 1997

My previous statements were made in haste. I was hungry
and confused, and I longed for purpose. I wanted to seem
like I was in the process of focusing in on something
important. I wanted to feel purpose rising like an ancient
city from the excavator's pick and shovel. I wanted this so
much that I rushed—I swung my pick wildly, and I brought
a great delicate city to the dust it had always verged on.

JUNE 29, 1997

Lifemeal causing pause. I am Mr. Frosty. I have chili in the unbuttfucked evening. If I had a wife, boy would I beat her. Didn't she ask for it? Wasn't she just begging for it? Anyone imagining that they are part of the lifemeal—how can they expect anything but a beating. I mean, am I to act as though a pause is what I wanted? I'd just as soon beat myself.

July 4, 1997 (Independence Day)

Who in their right mind wants the blood of uppity midgets
running down the walls and threatening the leisure of our
children? Who is so sleepy he can turn a deaf ear to the
steady growth of those midget-blood puddles? And do not
be deceived—the midgets do not die—the midgets *heal*
and return to the scene of their abuse. They are uppity.
The only thing for us to do is move.

JULY 6, 1997

Moisten the prickle a bit. Turn the volume down a tad. Loosen the restraints so I can almost not feel them. Instill purpose without disturbing resignation. Moisten the prickle a bit more. Feed me the volume like it was rare. Dismiss the seeming wake in the seasons. Instill hatred without lessening attention to detail. Restore the restraints.

JULY 7, 1997

The thing is, I have no real obligations. The moon shines,
the people circulate unto disappearance, the products
clarify themselves, and I am bound to tend to none of it. I
may be inclined, but I'm not bound. There's a difference.
In order to be bound, one has to pretend one has no special
interest in disappearing. One has to pretend there is no way
out. That pretending, mercifully, grows tired of itself.

JULY 8, 1997

Puny husbands discuss all the latest advances as the sun dies down. They do not lightly stroke one another's forearms, though their sentences attempt something similar. But they say the sentences aren't really theirs. They think a common mother speaks through them, and insodoing, lets them cause one another to be stroked. She keeps the discussion from ever arriving at its puny sources.

JULY 9, 1997

I'm so sorry for everything I've said. I'd take it back if I could. I am willing to admit that, in some sense, these descriptions of my visits have obscured the sufficiency of the meals I've had. I will not admit, however, that sufficiency is something I could be reasonably expected to live with. That is, I am truly sorry, but an insufficient meal *is* available, and nothing else tastes as sweet.

JULY 11, 1997

The menu's progress is glacial. Its merciless churning is no business of mine. No business of anyone. It is its own, only its own. It keeps its destination to itself. Or perhaps it does not know. Perhaps it just plods aimlessly into space. Perhaps it isn't progress at all but an obsessive circling-staggering over the same ground. No wonder somebody every now and then pees in the sink.

JULY 14, 1997

I will miss this spectacle. Sorely miss. I sorely miss it now. The children writhing on the floor, half-imagining how near they are to being set at ease. Meat induces sleep, they told me when I was a child, but what does sleep induce? Please accept my apology. It was never my intention to be actual.

JULY 16, 1997

The surgery lasting much longer than expected. I guess we sleep standing up, we surgeons. We sing softly to ourselves, if not to the patient. What use singing to the patient? We sing about not being able to tell day from night. We sing about closing up the body and going home. We sing in our sleep. The surgery seems further from an end, now, than it ever has before.

JULY 18, 1997

I was just minding the sweet strong bottoms of new customers. Why is it the bottoms of new customers always seem sweeter and stronger? Today I forced myself to eat a burger knowing full well I would not be able to keep it down. How useless I have become! How bottomless the mind!

JULY 19, 1997

Sickness I'm used to. I never write about it—the way I never write about my own face. But sickness is never only sickness; it grows, it improves itself, so that at certain points it seems a whole new thing. I am at such a point now. I've been sick in the past—steadily and truly—and yet, I am sick now in a way that makes me want to say that I was never sick at all, until here, until now.

JULY 20, 1997

My hair hurts. Tomorrow is all full of nods. These thorns do not become me, but that's alright.

JULY 22, 1997

To be dead in the summer-time is lucky. Summer-time is the best incinerator there is. I am easing in. My palpitation exposed, thready and pushed. The opposite of the blue sky, which impresses me, as unpushed as it is. A foreigner, the blue sky, in this land of panics, this land of incinerators. I would introduce myself, had I a name.

JULY 25, 1997

I am trying to refrain from decision, or from imagining myself as a Maker of decision. If I succeed, there will be a sense of gods, or God, or what is painfully equivalent. This sense is something to speak of. Until then, it's only money. Thank you for honoring mine all this time.

JULY 26, 1997

Now I lay me down to teeth—I drain the gruel my hole to keep—and if I should die before I quake—I say the drain my hole to take. Now I lay me down to feet—I brain the air my pain to treat—and if I should fuck before I wake—I sprain the eye my soul to take. (I pray bring me a softer booth!)

JULY 27, 1997

I am an actor at last. I can feel it. The camera on me, and the lights, and the audience. I suppose the audience isn't *on* me, not really — if I am indeed an actor, it is more accurate to say that I am on the audience. It feels good. It's all I've really ever wanted — to be carried off by people I don't know.

JULY 29, 1997

The walk, riddled with plank-light, resists my every proud seepage. And there are no tranq-baths, as I've said—just songs saying so. Huge sheets of paper thrown over everything that was left out in the open. I mean the generators—that is the term, I believe, *generators*—the generators from which the songs seep up. It's awkward, the walk through here, the walk toward the tranq-baths, which aren't.

August 2, 1997

When to unleash the stores? That has always been the question, but one really hears it when bones begin to ache. Still, it's a judgment call, like it always was. The next question is better: are the stores really open, or just what these here surfaces need to keep from always collapsing into merely shining? When I get to this question, I know it's time.

AUGUST 3, 1997

Numcrous bites — numerous. Having swimmed, having swimmed so far, so pale-facedly. White as a ghost. White as a ghost-bite—the one!! Terrible to see one's estate putting itself in order. Ghosts can't swim—it is very hard to picture it. And yet one feels the bites—one feels the bites indeed. The many.

August 7, 1997

Nonplussed. Nonplussed and recovering us. Recovering us even. Uneven. The brightnesses of it. All is light! Do you hear? Light.

THANKS TO

Romana Norton
Keshar Wenderoth
Brian Henry
Stuart Downs
Julianna Schmitt
Pete Lothringer
Heather McHugh
Graham Foust
Ruthe Thompson
Gabrielle Schmitt
Lupe Solis
Adrian Louis
Beaumont Slope
Eileen Thomas
Steve Berg
Matthew Zapruder
Tim Boehme

Karen Fish
Beth Weatherby
Leslie Stahlhut
Sandy Mosch
Larry Thanner III.
Chad Faries
Peter Ramos
Jesse Thanner
Bret Hughes
John D'Agata
Nerve.com
Nerve
American Poetry Review
Verse
Painted Bride Quarterly
Viacom

Joe Wenderoth's vitals can be found at www.versepress.org.